Here I Come—
Ready or Not

by Jean Merrill
and Frances Gruse Scott

ALBERT WHITMAN & COMPANY

CHICAGO

Second Printing 1975
Standard Book Number 8075-3244-4
Library of Congress Card Number 76-115897
Text © 1970 by Jean Merrill; Illustrations© 1970 by Frances Gruse Scott
Published simultaneously in Canada by George J. McLeod, Limited, Toronto
Lithographed in the United States of America

for Katy and Tony

"One—two—
three—four—
five—six—
seven—
eight—
nine—

TEN.

HERE
I
COME—

READY OR NOT!"

Katy is looking for Tony.
There are so many places to hide in a barn.

Katy looks in a horse stall.
No. Tony isn't there.

She looks in a manger.
Six baby cats!
But where is Tony?

Katy looks all around.
There's a trapdoor in the ceiling.
And there's one in the floor.

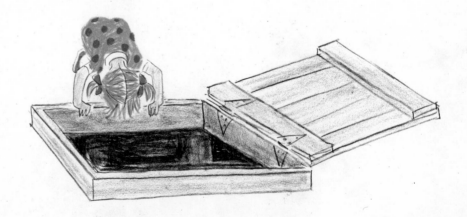

Oh, there's Tony—behind the bales of straw.

Now it's Katy's turn to hide.

"One—
     two—
   three—
        seven—
  four—

   TEN.

HERE I COME—

READY OR NOT!"

Tony looks behind crates.
Behind baskets and barrels.

Oh—*there's* Katy!

Tony's turn to hide.
"One—two—three—
four—five—six—

seven—eight—nine—TEN.

HERE I COME—

READY

OR

NOT!"

Where is Tony this time?
Could he be in the haymow?
Yes, he could.
But will Katy ever find him?

She found him!

Now Tony has to look.
He looks in the feed room.

Is Katy in the feed bin?
Or behind the feed bags?
Where can she be?

Ah, *there* she is.

Now Tony finds a funny place to hide.
He pretends he is a cow.

But Katy finds him right away
He doesn't look like a cow.

Then Katy finds the best place.
Tony can't find her.

"I'm inside," Katy calls.
"But you can see me from outside."

But Tony can't find her anywhere.

"Do you give up?" Katy calls.

"Yes," Tony says. "I give up."

"Look up," calls Katy. "Up, up, UP!"

Then it's time for lunch.

You get very hungry hiding in a barn.

"Lunch is ready," says Mother.
"Are you READY OR NOT?"

"We're READY!" says Tony.

The End